I CHOOSE *You*

I CHOOSE You

CHIDINMA ONWENI, MD

Printed in the United States of America
Published in Hellertown, PA
Cover design by Kim Lewis
Photo on page 14 by Alive Films
Wedding photos by Fotos by Fola
Headshots by Jacqueline Agentis
Library of Congress Control Number 2025925483
ISBN paperback 979-8-89420-075-0
ISBN eBook 979-8-89420-076-7
For more information or to place bulk orders,
contact the author or the publisher at Jennifer@
BrightCommunications.net.

To my daughter, Rainbow: We are grateful that you chose us to be your parents.

To Dr. Jason Siegel, thank you for always being there, for always listening.

To Dr. William D. Freeman, thank you for shining the light to emulate the path for others.

Contents

Foreword

By Dr. Marlena Fejzo

In every life, there are moments that bend time—when a single decision carves a canyon between who we were and who we must become. *I Choose You* is a memoir of one woman's journey through such moments—painful, messy, deeply human moments—where the choices weren't easy, and the consequences weren't clean. But they were hers.

Dr. Chidinma's story is not a linear arc of triumph. It is a raw, unflinching portrait of what it means to choose between career and body, expectation and reality, survival and surrender. At every turn, she was asked to pick: the path of least resistance or the one forged in fire. And she chose. Over and over again. She chose when there was no good option, when the cost of each path was unbearable, when every decision carved a deeper wound.

Dr. Chidinma chose to stay in the room with pain. She chose to keep showing up to a job that misunderstood her, to a body that betrayed her, to a pregnancy that nearly killed her. She chose to advocate for herself when medicine failed. She chose to be vulnerable enough to admit what helped—even when science disapproved. She chose to tell the truth, even when it was ugly, even when it was inconvenient. And when the choice became life or death, she chose herself. She chose her child. She chose love.

What makes this story extraordinary is not that the author survived hyperemesis gravidarum. It's how she did it—with spit cups and science, with mangoes and melons, with faith and fear side by side. With deep love for a child who had not yet arrived, and for a husband who whispered, "I choose you," when the world went quiet.

This is not a book about pregnancy. It's a book about power. About reclaiming it when it slips away. About rewriting what it means to be strong. About learning from gut wrenching experience and sharing the lessons. And about how sometimes the bravest thing a woman can do is say: *I choose me.*

As you read this book, prepare to be cracked open. You'll witness the impossible math of survival. You'll see a woman make choices no one should have to make—and live to tell you why she made them.

Marlena Fejzo, PhD, Clinical Assistant professor of Population and Public Health Sciences in the Center for Genetic Epidemiology Keck School of Medicine, University of Southern California

Chapter 1: The Wedding

The year 2023 was a busy one with two weddings on two different continents, a new job, a new house, a new state. This was the year I thought would usher in celebration, rest, and finally, joy. But it had other plans. And I, always the planner, was the last one to loosen my grip.

The Nigerian wedding was a dream I didn't know I needed. My eldest sister, the matriarch in spirit if not in years, took the reins and orchestrated everything like a general who had nothing to prove but everything to deliver. Every flower was placed, every dance timed to the beat of our lineage. I didn't have to micromanage. I didn't have to panic. I was allowed to be the bride. I was at the center, not the coordinator. And that, in hindsight, felt like a once-in-a-lifetime gift.

In my family, we say, "Nothing lost, nothing missing, everyone accounted for."

And on that day, it wasn't just a motto; it was a spiritual truth.

Then came the American wedding. I approached it like a case with a complex diagnosis. I obsessed over every vendor, every flower, and every email as if they were the symptoms I had to monitor. Then I prescribed the perfect remedy, and I wanted the day to whisper love from every corner. I wanted Auntie Ethel's voice—"Where there are flowers, there is love"—to echo in every bloom, every petal, and every scent.

But when the day finally arrived, the cure didn't happen. The florist did not deliver the promised amount of flowers. The lighting flared too cold. The church walk-in song was wrong and poorly cued. As the church bells chimed, my sister, Ngozi, vanished. Later, I learned she'd slipped outside, a desperate silhouette against the stormy sky, arms raised as if to bargain with the heavens. I thought the downpour had merely ruined the nonexistent cocktail hour. Now, I wonder if it wasn't a sign. God, we had a deal. So why the rain? Even today if I look at the photos, I'm smiling— but I remember the sweat behind the veil. Maybe these were the side effects that I had to endure.

In the days that followed, I did not honeymoon—I autopsied. Every missed cue replayed in my head like a courtroom trial, and I was both the accused and the executioner. It was something more tender, and somehow worse; it was disappointment. The moment that I'd been imagining since girlhood had come and gone abruptly. It had felt incomplete. But Jacob, my husband, tried his best. He tried to pull me into joy. He rubbed my back and said, "We're married. That's the only detail that matters." But I couldn't hear him over the sound of my own expectations crashing.

Then, just as the dust of disappointment began to settle and I promised myself a fresh start—more sex, less stress, no more control-freak planning—the universe smirked. A stick turned pink. A clock rewound. I was six weeks pregnant. And just like that, I realized: While I was trying to relive a wedding that had already passed, life had quietly moved on inside me. Joy had knocked on the door I wasn't even facing.

Lesson: Live in the moment. Do not postpone joy. Surrender to the "now." Do what you want right now, and be done with it. Weddings are seen as "perfect" moments in both American and Nigerian traditions. We gave it our all. It was time to move on. I was trying to "earn" joy through perfection, instead of living it. The lesson I carry forward is one of surrender, releasing the need for perfect plans, and living in the present. Learning surrender now becomes a prelude to the many surrenders of motherhood.

Chapter 2: Food Poisoning

We met at one of those neutral cafés that tries too hard—white plates, concrete floors, rosemary on everything. I chose a table that seemed empty but also somewhat welcoming. I ordered flatbread I wouldn't taste. My stomach was already tight knotted from the email subject line: *Lunch? Need to talk*.

The unit medical director sat across from me, smiling with lips but not eyes. She waited until the drinks arrived before dropping it: "I've heard some feedback about you. Words like… 'intimidating,' 'harsh,' even 'unapproachable.'"

Then she took another sip and sat with her back straight. She kept her drink on the table and continued with her talk. But to me each word was a blow dressed in civility. They landed sharp as needles, thin and pointy, designed to pierce without drawing blood. I swallowed hard, feeling both insulted and cornered. I wanted to ask: *Do they call the men harsh? Or is assertiveness only ugly on women like me?* But I smiled warmly, nodding gently to show my understanding. I stayed silent, allowing her to finish speaking without interruption.

"Thank you for letting me know," I heard myself say.

The check came moments later, and I left the café with that flatbread still lodged in my throat like a silent protest.

That night, I couldn't sleep. The sheets were tangled, but my thoughts were even worse. I told myself it was the stress or maybe the flatbread. But the bitterness in my mouth wasn't from the arugula. By morning, my gut was at war. I was cramping hard, diarrhea came so sudden that it almost scared me, and waves of nausea surrounded my body. I told myself it was food poisoning, because anything else—anything deeper— would mean stopping. And I couldn't stop. Not now. Not with a new job, a new city, a reputation already under scrutiny.

I also thought that the discomfort could be a physical manifestation of the upset and disappointment from the stressful lunch. *Bitterness in the body often begins as bitterness in the mind,* I kept on telling myself. But the discomfort continued and started to get worse. By day three, I couldn't even stand long enough to brush my teeth. My limbs trembled, my belly roared, and I told myself that it had to be food poisoning. I walked into the emergency room (ER) for evaluation.

Under fluorescent lights, sterile smells, stiff bedsheets, and emotional claustrophobia, everything felt overexposed. I was still wearing my work badge—proof that I belonged somewhere, even if my body disagreed. The physician introduced herself with kindness I wasn't prepared for. She asked about my symptoms, my job, and if I'd eaten anything strange.

Then she asked, "Any chance you could be pregnant?"

"No," I said reflexively. Then hesitated. "I mean … probably not." She smiled, tapped on the keyboard.

"Let's find out anyway." While waiting, she wheeled in a small bedside ultrasound machine. "Let's take a look," she said, her voice like velvet.

Seconds later, a grainy black-and-white flicker appeared.

"There it is," she whispered.

There what is? The question barely formed before the answer appeared on the screen. At first, it was just a grainy blur, shifting with the movement of the probe, but then I saw it too. A tiny sac, so impossibly small yet holding the weight of an entire new reality. I couldn't speak. The words simply dissolved somewhere between my chest and my lips. I couldn't even blink. A sound came out that was somewhere between a laugh and a scream. I began to cry.

But the doctor's hand was warm when it rested gently on my arm. Her voice, low and certain, cut through the rushing in my eyes.

"It's okay," she murmured, as if speaking directly to the part of me that was bracing for impact. "Jobs are replaceable. Families aren't. You'll be okay."

Her words sank in slowly, but I wasn't ready to be okay. I wanted to believe her. I really did. But right then, belief was too heavy to lift.

My phone buzzed and lit up with a video call from my sister in Nigeria. I stared at the screen, my breath caught, and my heart raced. I didn't answer because saying it out loud would make it real. But her timing wasn't a coincidence. In our family, pain travels. It doesn't need visas and flies across oceans on breath and blood, without a passport.

Jacob and I went home. We could not go to the town festival we had planned for. I was too sick and sad to go anywhere. I kept on saying to myself, *I didn't even get to have the wild sex.* Not only was I pregnant, but these symptoms seemed severe. I already felt sick, not just from body but homesick as well. I missed my family, and I thought about if I should call back my sister or not. But above all, I hoped it will would subside soon, or maybe it would only happen in the mornings, as the name suggests "morning sickness."

Lesson: This chapter wasn't just about a misdiagnosed stomachache. It was about all the ways we misdiagnose transformation—as failure, as shame, as something to hide. I thought it was food poisoning, an inconvenience I could push through with enough rest and over-the-counter remedies. But it was the beginning of a new life. One that terrified me. One I hadn't asked for, and one that came with a weight I wasn't ready to carry.

And yet, there it was—growing *in spite* of me. Claiming space inside a body too tired to fight back. And inside me it whispered: Ready or not, I'm already here.

Note: The formal name of this pregnancy illness will be introduced in the following chapters.

Chapter 3: ER

I stopped keeping count of how many times I vomited. Mornings bled into evenings in a haze of bile and exhaustion. My esophagus felt raw and peeled back. I couldn't keep down water, couldn't lie down for longer hours, couldn't think in full thoughts without retching.

At first, I thought if I simply emptied everything—if there was nothing left—my body would stop. But it didn't. Even when there was no food, no water, and no electrolytes left to give, my body still found something to eject. First it was yellow, and then clear. After that, it was followed by pain. People call it morning sickness. But this was something else. This was a siege, and by nightfall, I felt like a refugee inside my own body.

But my medical brain wouldn't turn off. I lay curled on the bathroom floor, phone in hand, scrolling through journal articles on thiamine deficiency, metabolic stress, and hyperemesis protocols. I felt I wasn't just a patient—I was a patient who knew better. And that offered its own kind of torture. When I returned to the ER, I felt the usual kind of suffocation, the lights, the antiseptic, the clipped voices of people. I saw the hospital bed that smelled like bleach and fatigue— the same fatigue that was my companion nowadays. I tried not to glance around much and focus all my senses only on myself.

I asked for thiamine, and the attending physician blinked at me. "We don't use that here for pregnancy nausea," she said, half polite and half dismissive.

"You should," I said softly. "You're going to see more of this."

She nodded politely. She gave me IV fluids. But this was not what I asked for, also a discharge paper that promised monitoring and follow-up—as if nausea listened to prescriptions.

I replied with a thank you, but inwardly, something split. I wasn't angry but rather disoriented. I myself was a doctor, and I'd just been dismissed like someone who didn't know her body. I left with numb arms and a heart that felt like it needed to do something soon.

I made a desperate appointment with the OB-GYN office. I must have sounded like a storm in a teacup on the phone because the lady on the other side did everything she could to fit me in. When I met the OB, she was the first who didn't flinch, her eyes scanning the ultrasound like a battlefield general surveying a wounded landscape, assessing damage with utmost precision.

"Just one," she said, eyes on the screen. "And that one is giving you hell." She didn't sugarcoat it. She scheduled me for tri-weekly infusions—at the cancer center, no less.

For me, it felt like an irony that landed hard. I sat near patients fighting for their lives and some counting down the end of theirs. The wait there and the uncertain eye contacts ran a shiver down my spine. And there I realized that their pain was much more than mine.

Then one day I was vomiting so much that I started having blood-tinged vomit followed by esophageal spasm and burning. The first time blood came up, Jacob ran. Not away from me. He sprinted to the kitchen, looking for towels, ice, and logic.

"We're going to the hospital," he said. His voice cracked like something sacred had split.

"No," I whispered. "Not again." I didn't want to wait in another waiting room. Another sympathetic face pretending to be helpful. Another round of "we'll just monitor you." I bargained with him: "If it happens again. If it gets worse." But the truth is, it was already bad. I simply wished to prevent others from seeing it.

I went to my first multivitamin infusion appointment. I was very nauseous, vomited several times, and noticed that the Zofran actually made me feel worse. After finishing my infusion, I went home. After so long I felt alive, like a new being.

As my husband described it, "You look jacked up, like you got 'your fix.'"

I boarded a plane and flew to North Carolina for my friend's wedding. I even enjoyed the dinner. But by Sunday, the storm clouds of my ailment began to gather again, symptoms returning like relentless waves crashing ashore. The journey back home was a voyage through treacherous waters, and I started to feel the sickness creeping in once more. Monday felt like a distant lighthouse, promising solace with my next infusion, a beacon guiding me through the darkness.

This time, I told them not to give me the Zofran, just the infusion. The ladies at these clinics were kind. Each person gave me suggestions on what to try at home, brands to consider, and one lady specifically recommended a hard candy. I tried it, didn't vomit, so I went home and bought a whole bag along with many other things from the website. But it was a dead end again. None of their suggestions worked.

The infusions helped me stand. They helped hydrate me a little, but it seemed they could not keep up with the amount of fluid I was losing. Finding a vein for the infusion was a struggle. They came at me with warm packs and optimism. I have small veins to begin with, now that they were all dehydrated, they could not be found, multiple sticks, multiple attempts, different nurses trying, and using a device that helps find veins.

"Tiny veins, huh? We'll get it."

But they didn't. Stick after stick. One nurse, then another. I watched the quiet shift in their faces—hope replaced by embarrassment.

"Can you please bring the ultrasound?" I begged. "I can't take this anymore."

They didn't. Eventually, a vein gave up its hiding place. But my arm looked like a battlefield.

During one of the follow-up labs, when I rolled up my sleeve, the lab technician flinched. He gave me a look that I had seen before. It was the look we give to IV illicit drug users because of the appearance of their arms. My arm was now looking like "drug popping" individuals.

As he stared just long enough at my arms, trying to figure out how and from where he would draw the blood, he asked, "What do you do for work?"

I knew why he was asking. He was trying to see how much respect to give me, how to judge me. We are guilty of this. We ask people what they do for work so we can gauge how to judge them.

"I am a physician," I replied. And everything changed. He adjusted his look, his demeanor, and his language mid-sentence "Sorry, doc, what happened?"

"I am pregnant and have hyperemesis gravidarum," I told him as I stared at the needle.

"I go to infusion clinic three times a week. Because I am so dry, my veins are hard to find. These marks and bruises are from multiple IV attempts."

In that moment, I wasn't a suffering woman. I was a profession. And that bought me dignity. I felt compassion from him, as he tried to draw my blood. We both cheered in relief when the blood started flowing into the tubing. Illness rewrites one's identity. I was no longer "doctor," I was "the girl with the track marks."

At this point, during my following OB-GYN appointment, I have lost nine pounds. I used Uber and Lyft for my appointment because I couldn't drive due to my weakness. Jacob had gone back to work; he couldn't keep missing work to drive me to these appointments. I want to thank Jacob's employers for the compassion and understanding. Still, I couldn't help noticing how his employers showed him more concern and flexibility than mine.

Every ride was its own small act of surrender, sliding into the backseat with my vomit bags and spit cups, hoping the driver wouldn't flinch or make a face. I want to thank the Uber and Lyft drivers, as well as all the strangers who became part of my survival story. Thank you for not rejecting the ride when you saw me clutching a plastic bag or when the smell of sickness lingered. Thank you for treating me like a person and not a burden.

At first, the infusions were magic. It was as if someone had plugged me back into a socket. But eventually, the magic dulled.

After each session, I felt worse—not better. A fellow doctor quietly suggested the reason: "You're at a cancer center. The air, the smell—it's grief. Your body knows it."

He was right. My stomach turned as soon as I stepped into that building. Not because of the drugs. But because of the cancer and chemo I could smell on the walls.

When I returned to work, the infusion clinic in the same building as my work was always full, and I could not drive far to another location in the middle of a workday, so I stopped all together.

Jacob sat on the bathroom floor with me. He didn't say anything at first and just watched my body convulse. He saw my glassy eyes and how I caught my breath between retches. He hurried away and brought water. He tried cold compresses as he kneeled beside me.

At one point, I looked over at him and saw his face cracked open. His eyes were too wide, and his lips were trembling like he wanted to speak but kept quiet. And instead of speaking, he placed a hand on the back of my neck to fix my position and give me support.

And in that moment, all I could hear barely above a whisper was:

"I hate watching you disappear."

Lesson: Hyperemesis gravidarum is not morning sickness. It is not something you power through with ginger tea and affirmations. It is a physiological prison. And without thiamine—a cheap, simple vitamin—your brain begins to starve.

Hyperemesis gravidarum patients need thiamine, in any form that they can tolerate. Thiamine should not be delayed. Do not wait for worsening symptoms or MRI findings. Getting the thiamine and IV fluid made me feel alive again. And it was the worst irony because I knew what I needed, but I still couldn't access it. The lesson here isn't just medical. It's moral. Listen to women. Believe them. Treat the pain you can't see. Don't wait to know their profession before you offer compassion.

Chapter 4: Spit Cup

I walked into work with a spit cup like it was a badge of shame. It wasn't elegant. It wasn't medical-grade. It was just a cup—clear plastic, paper-lined, whatever I could grab. It was tucked inside my jacket sleeve but still visible, still loud, even when I said nothing.

It came with me into patient rooms, meetings, and charting huddles. At first, I tried to hide it. Then I stopped trying. Every few seconds: spit, swallow, gag. Spit again. I felt the silence of some people around me, as they stared. Some asked, while others didn't. Others gave sideways glances, like I was violating some professional hygiene code.

One day a resident leaned over my shoulder to look at a scan I was reviewing. I spoke—low and fast, explaining a CT finding—and he physically jumped back. I knew immediately. It wasn't what I said.

It was my breath. Hyperemesis didn't just rob me of food and dignity. It robbed me of closeness.

I felt a lack of support, like people thought, "Every woman has had morning sickness. Why is yours any different?"

"Try Zofran."

"My wife had that. She just pushed through."

"Ginger tea. Works wonders."

"Why can't you complete your shift?

"Do you have to be off from work?" Everyone had a remedy, but only few offered empathy. I started to resent the phrase "morning sickness." It sounded so manageable, so mild. This wasn't a morning thing. It was an all-hours purge. There were days I didn't feel pregnant; I felt possessed.

By then, I had lost eleven pounds. I looked skeletal in a work jacket that once fit me like armor. Now, I draped it like a costume.

Jacob is a mechanical engineer, so I encouraged him to create a device I could spit into, that won't be so obvious, something that could attach to my hip or wrist so I wouldn't have to carry a cup around. I watched Jacob sketch on napkins, scroll hardware catalogs, mumble things like "elastic tubing" and "hands-free spout."

We brainstormed a design together—much like parents planning a future. A discreet tube under my shirt. A valve to release the saliva into a container at my waist. Something that didn't scream disabled. He ordered parts. Prototypes arrived in Amazon boxes. But he never finished it. And I never blamed him. Maybe the world wasn't ready for a woman who needed a wearable spit reservoir. But I was. So, I continued to use a cup or a bag throughout the pregnancy.

I thought about tossing the cup. Crumpling it, burying it deep in the trash, but I didn't. This was what helped me survive. That ugly little cup caught what my body refused to hold. It wasn't heroic, but it was practical. It didn't heal me, but it honored the truth that I was not okay.

Lesson: I will continue to bother Jacob about this spit device because I believe that future patients with hyperemesis gravidarum will benefit from it.

We measure pain in relativity. "If I survived it, you should too." "If I didn't complain, neither should you." But suffering isn't a relay race. It's not comparative.

The same diagnosis wears different faces, different screams. I still struggle to remember this—still catch myself judging others with my own yardstick. But that spit cup taught me something: If it makes you feel better, carry it with pride. Even if the whole world winces when they see you lift it to your lips.

Chapter 5: Thirst

I watched people drink from their cups, mugs, and water bottles like it was nothing—like swallowing was a quiet privilege no one announced. The cold condensation on the outside of their cups looked obscene in its simplicity. That slick, sweating glass. That proof that relief existed.

I wanted a taste, just one. But I already knew my body wouldn't cooperate. It wasn't thirst the way people mean it. It was thirst for normal. For the casual act of taking in water and trusting it would stay.

One day at work, I watched a nurse sip from her drink between tasks, unbothered, steady, like nausea was an occasional inconvenience instead of a full-time occupation. It took everything in me not to ask her for a sip. And the sick part is, I don't even think it was the sip I wanted. It was the sweat on the cup. The coldness. The promise.

Then there was the other truth I didn't notice until it became impossible to ignore.

I had not urinated in days.

It sounds dramatic written out like that. It didn't feel dramatic in the moment. It felt… logical. If nothing was staying in, nothing could come out. My body was a place where input had become a rumor.

After the ER visit, after the IV fluid boluses, my body finally produced something. When I went, it was dark—too dark—just a few ounces, like my kidneys were rationing whatever was left of me. I can't remember the smell. Maybe my brain filed it away under trauma and locked the drawer.

Lesson: Hyperemesis makes you doubt what's real. If you're living inside it and you realize you haven't peed in days, you are not weak. You are not exaggerating. Your body has nothing to give because everything is coming out of your mouth. It is still serious. It still deserves medical attention. But you are not imagining the severity.

This is what thirst looks like when it's not poetic.

It's quiet. It's humiliating.

And it is terrifying.

Chapter 6: Melon

It started with one bite. The cool, soft, sweet like relief. I waited. Five minutes. Ten. And then an hour. There was no gag, no traces of bile. I felt no betrayal. I tried different food items and drinks, looking for something that would stay down and not end up in vomit. But over this one, I cried.

Green cantaloupe melon was the winner. I had it chilled, right out of the refrigerator and no sprint to the bathroom. I was totally stunned.

Jacob didn't say anything. He simply walked back to the kitchen and cut another half. That night, we called her Melon.

"Our Melon baby." A silly name. But also, a sacred one.

Every day, I'd whisper to her, "Let's keep it down today, okay?" And some days, she listened. And if it stayed down, I savored a lot. Melon was doing well and growing, despite what was going on with me, Glory to God.

Jacob would say, "I have never cut this amount of melons in my life."

But he would still happily bring a full bowl of chilled melons and place it like a sacred offering. There's something unspeakable holy about finding one thing your betraying body allows you to consume. Melon became my daily ritual, sliced carefully, and I swallowed it slowly. I could taste the sweetness. I could sit upright, and I could imagine a world where the tide of nausea wouldn't devour me every day at sunrise.

Like all false gods, melon betrayed me. One morning, I bit in, the bite I'd taken a dozen times before, slid down but within seconds, I was on the floor again. I felt violent heaves of acidic rage and blood-tinged foam.

"No," I whispered. "Not you too."

I tried again. This time a different melon. A riper one. A colder one and same result. Melon was gone, and above all, I lost another promise. The thing that kept me tethered to life… had let go. When I ate it, I vomited.

Why? Why did it stop working? It was my food and my water. It helped lubricate my lips that had torn in many areas. We were back to square one of looking for what I could keep down.

I reached my OB-GYN for help and asked what to try. We had tried all anti-nausea/vomiting medication orally, intravenously, and rectally.

Recently, Jacob reminded me of the first time he helped me with the rectal anti-nausea medication. How he felt so sorry for me and hoped that this route would work, only to see me vomiting again and pooping at the same time. Nothing helped me.

My OB-GYN stated, "If you can make it to ten weeks then we can do IV steroid." IV steroids before 10 weeks carries a possible risk of cleft palate in babies.

Ten weeks could not come fast enough. During that time, I was tired and almost ready to give up. One day I found myself on the floor and crying. It started as a whisper.

"Are you okay?" the question sounded serious even as he said it.

I blurted, "Just kill me now."

Soon, it became background music. "I can't do this. I want to die." I said it again in the bathroom, on the floor with my back against the cold tile, with my head resting on the rim of the tub. I said it between gulps of air. I said it without realizing I was saying it—like breathing.

The light in the bathroom was dim, but it still hurt my eyes. My skin felt as though it had been drained of fluids. I could feel my heart thumping way louder, not because I was afraid but because my body was running on fumes. But this was a scene I was used to.

One day, Jacob came in quietly, so quietly I didn't hear him at first. He knelt beside me, the floor creaking under his weight. Out of the corner of my eye, I caught his knees on the tile, the way his hands hesitated before reaching toward me as if approaching wild grief. He smelled lightly of laundry detergent. He tilted his head, looking at me in a way that made my chest ache.

He then lifted my chin, and said: "I choose you." Those were just three words, but to me it was one miracle. He said it again, much slower this time. His words felt like a vow.

"You don't have to keep going for her, or for me. But I choose you. If you want to stop, we'll stop. But I need you to know—I choose you and will always do."

And for the first time, I felt chosen. Not because I was pregnant. Not because I was surviving. Just because I was me.

The words didn't heal me instantly, and the vomiting didn't stop. Also, the exhaustion didn't lift, but something definitely shifted.

Many times I thought, *I wish we still lived in the prior state because there were tall buildings I could jump off from.* Sometimes while driving, I searched for tall buildings. Then one day it occurred to me that the tallest building is my workplace. Then I thought, *I should do it the next time I am in that building.*

Other times, I thought, *Thank God we live in a state that allows pregnancy termination.* But Jacob's words "I choose you" gave me strength.

I blinked slowly, tears mixed with sweat, trying to process those three words. He said this, not "we'll survive this" or "get better soon," just "I choose you."

Choosing means selecting or picking out (someone or something) as the best or most suitable among two or more options. Jacob was choosing me and rejecting the alternative, whatever that might be.

I stopped saying "kill me now" and "I want to die." It was the last time I said those words. The phrase "I choose you" got me through. When I feel tired, I think of "I choose you." When I feel like giving up, I remember "I choose you." I started to say it myself, "I choose you." "I choose you, Chidinma." "I choose you, Melon."

Lesson: Try different food items to see which food item you can keep down. As my OB-GYN said, This is not a time to try to eat healthy, eat whatever you can keep down.

Also, words are powerful. Sometimes a simple hug can do. Words saved me where medicine couldn't. A dozen IV drips didn't give me what one sentence from Jacob did. There are people who think language is soft, less than science. But I know better. "I choose you" became my mantra. My breath. My anchor. Later, when doctors adjusted meds, when melons failed, when spit cups filled—I repeated it. I choose you,

Chidinma. I choose you, Melon. Melon stopped working, but I kept the nickname. Because even when sweetness turns sour, you cling to the memory of the sugar. Because if no one else chooses you, you must choose yourself.

Sometimes, a few encouraging words can save a life and help someone get through a difficult time. In my case, it was a simple "I choose you."

I know there are women who have ended up terminating their pregnancy due to severe hyperemesis gravidarum. Please remember that termination is not a treatment of hyperemesis gravidarum. I hope you find relief, hope, and support, so termination can be off the table.

https://www.hyperemesis.org/wp-content/uploads/2017/09/Taylor-research-prednisolone-treatment-2009.pdf

Chapter 7: Steroid

By week ten, I was paper-thin—bones and bile in a hospital gown. I walked into the ER wrapped in Jacob's hoodie because I couldn't bear the weight of fabric against my skin. The admitting nurse looked at me with alarm.

"You're the hyperemesis patient?" I nodded. She didn't ask questions—just wheeled me in past the waiting room into the fluorescent core of the ward. The air had a particular scent of "in-between," which can be described as being between sick and discharged, between hope and lost.

They started fluids and IV vitamins that went in after a few attempts. Then came the steroid drip. I closed my eyes. Not in prayer. Not in sleep. But in fear—*What if this doesn't work either?*

The next morning, my OB walked into the hospital room with her usual crisp confidence. She took one look at me and froze.

"She smiles!" she gasped, hands flying to her chest like she'd seen a miracle. We both laughed. Or maybe only I did. She said, "This is the first time I've seen you smile." And it was truly genuine. I hadn't smiled in weeks, maybe even months—not a real one, at least. This smile felt different; it came from a place beyond words, a moment of stillness, like a brief pause amid a storm.

"Are you hungry?" she asked.

I paused. I wasn't sure what that word meant anymore. "I don't know," I said. "But I want to try."

She helped me order cream of wheat. A strange comfort food. Plain. Soft. I lifted the spoon as if it were a ritual. The first bite felt like permission to live. And it stayed down. I didn't cry. I wanted to, but my body had no spare tears.

At 3 a.m., I called my cousin. I hadn't spoken to her in weeks. Maybe longer. She answered on the first ring. "I'm pregnant," I said. "And I'm in the hospital. I just kept vomiting and couldn't eat for months. But now… I want white rice and chicken sauce."

She didn't ask questions. She just said, "I'll be there." When she arrived, she brought enough food for a week. She told me her own story with hyperemesis gravidarum.

"That's why I only had two kids," she said. "The second nearly killed me." We sat together like two survivors trading scars in the dark.

She encouraged me and said "This will be over soon, and your baby will soon be lying beside you."

I cried. I felt encouraged. This could be genetic. But then a different thought crept in. *Why haven't the women in my family talked about this? How did they all do this and survive?* My mother, my grandmothers, my aunts—how did they endure it? And if they suffered, why did they never speak of it? Was it pride or maybe protection? Or was it simply swallowed whole, filed away as something not worth mentioning because "every women goes through it?"

Then shame followed close behind. Am I the weakest one? The words echo like an accusation. Weakness isn't supposed to be in my bloodline. I felt like I was falling into something that women in my family did quietly, without applause, without ever needing to say, "It's hard."

Soon, the steroid helped me, and I started eating a little bit, here and there, mostly plain white boiled rice. After the large steroid doses in the hospital. I was discharged with a steroid taper to take at home.

By the time I left the hospital, I was swollen. My cheeks, my ankles, my feet. I didn't recognize myself in the mirror. It wasn't weight—it was water and hormones and desperation. I stopped the taper early. I knew I wasn't supposed to. But I wanted to reclaim my face, my body, something. The swelling faded. Slowly. But the memory of those moon-shaped cheeks haunted me. I looked like someone else. I felt like someone else.

That's the thing about survival: It doesn't always make you feel whole. Sometimes, it just makes you feel… swollen. I believe it is because of the steroid and the amount of IV fluid I received while at the hospital. When I returned home after stopping the taper early, my swollen face, legs, and feet resolved.

Lesson: Steroids are not salvation. They are tools. But tools can be heavy. They gave me my appetite back. They gave me a few peaceful days without making me think that I'm weak. But they also changed my face. Made me fear the mirror. And yet—when you've been drowning, even a leaky raft is a blessing. Relief doesn't have to be pretty. It just has to keep you afloat.

For hyperemesis gravidarum, current recommendations suggest limiting use of steroids prior to ten weeks of pregnancy because there may be a risk of cleft palate, but more studies are needed.

Chapter 8: Night Shift

Before pregnancy, night shifts were annoying. Inconvenient. Now, they were apocalyptic. The lights felt harsher. The hospital hallways colder. The hours longer, more surreal. The overhead lights buzzed louder at 3 a.m.

During the day, I could pretend I was okay. But at night, my body rebelled in silence—when everyone else's pain took priority. The nausea sharpened after midnight. My head throbbed. And every hour closer to dawn, my resolve cracked. I vomited more during the night shifts and the mornings after. It was brutal, and every step I took echoed fatigue.

On one night shift since melon has stopped working for me, I needed hydration, but water betrayed me. Juice was too thick. Ginger ale was too sweet. And then I remembered Coca-Cola. Not for the taste but for the fizz.

I purchased a bottle from the hospital vending machine. Then I went for another. The carbonation hit the back of my throat like a reset button. For a few minutes, I felt as if everything was fine. And for another few minutes, I felt … possible. So I drank two, and it got converted into too many. But I remained, unraveling with the patients. I spit bile into cups and took patient notes effortlessly. The smell of antiseptic made me gag, but I still moved room to room, nodding like I could still do it all because you are not allowed to stop wearing the coat. Everyone's watching; everyone's counting on you. But by the time the shift ended, I was vomiting again. Violently. But I didn't regret it because for two hours, I was free.

When the morning team arrived, one of my coworkers saw the empty bottle of Coca-Cola in the trash can and celebrated. "Hey you drank something." I said yes, but did not see the need to state that I had been vomiting since drinking that bottle.

On the way to the car, I took a detour to the staff bathroom at the end of the hallway. I barely made it. The retching started before I could close the door. Violent. Animalistic. Someone walked in, then walked right back out. I heard her whispering outside, "Something's wrong in there." Seconds later, another woman entered—older, softer.

"Are you okay?" she asked, her voice cautious but kind.

"Just throwing up," I whispered.

She handed me a paper towel, and for that moment, I could've cried. Not from pain—but from being seen.

The next morning, I reached out to the doctor in charge of making the schedules. Not as a doctor. Not as a hero. As a woman on the edge of collapse.

"Can we reduce my night shifts? Just a little?"

In this profession, we're trained to push through, to serve before we self-care, to bury suffering in logic and layers of institutional pride.

But he agreed. Two in a row instead of four. And I realized something: Even small asks are revolutionary when you're trained to never speak up.

Lesson: The carbonation of Coca-Cola was what initially helped. The secret wasn't in the sugar but in the bubbles— carbonation, movement, lightness. I craved these, not just physically but spiritually.

The high sugar content likely caused my violent vomiting. Discovering a non-sugar carbonated drink was crucial and a real game changer for me.

I remembered Heineken, that it is bitter and carbonated and has a non-alcoholic version. That became my drink, few sips a day, not too much.

Later, Jacob found a drink at a gas station: Topo Chico mineralized water. I took a sip. It stayed down. For weeks, it was my ritual. My communion. I drank one every morning like a prayer. Not too fast. Not too much. But just enough to say: I am still here. The bottle was slim. Clear. Elegant. It didn't demand anything of me. It didn't scream heal. It simply fizzed. Softly. And that's what I needed—something that didn't force hope. Just offered it.

Another important lesson I learned from my bathroom experience with the woman running out is: Whenever you see or hear someone in distress, take a moment to stop and ask if they're okay or if they need help. A little kindness can go a long way!

Chapter 9: Admission

By the second day of my hospital admission, my chest ached like something inside me had fractured. Each breath was shallow and hesitant, as if my lungs were unsure whether they wanted to continue working. I called the nurse with a voice that barely cleared my throat.

"I think I'm drowning inside," I told her.

She turned and looked at me. She came closer, but this time, not like a patient with morning sickness, but like someone standing on the edge of a cliff.

She checked my vitals and called the doctors. They ran an EKG. I knew the signs, so I asked them to stop the fluids. Within hours, the pain faded. It wasn't just my body that was overwhelmed. It was everything.

My work administration scheduled a meeting while I was in a hospital bed, still connected to an IV. They called to assure me I wouldn't be fired and that I would keep my job while I was ill. I paused to process their message, and the silence grew awkward until I realized they were waiting for me to express gratitude.

I whispered the words, "Thank you, I appreciate it" not because I meant it, but because I knew the cost of not saying it.

They wanted me to be grateful to them for keeping my job. I was grateful, but I was lying in a hospital bed. My job was the last thing on my mind on this day. Where was the compassion? The concern? Even the pretense—"Do you want us to send someone to check on you?" But no. All they wanted was compliance dressed as gratitude.

One of the nurses came in to check my vitals. She was quiet and kind. She looked at the bags under my eyes, the IV lines, the spit cup.

"I had it too," she said. It was the first time someone in scrubs looked at me and didn't see a problem to solve—but a sister in survival. She told me about B_6 and doxylamine. Said it saved her. In her voice, I heard hope. And something else. Permission to ask for help.

The next morning, when my OB came in for rounds, I asked. Not as a doctor. Not even as a patient. As a woman who was ready to keep living.

"Can I try B_6 and doxylamine?"

She said yes. That was the moment I realized I could speak, ask questions, and be heard. It was something I already knew about, but still hesitated to request. Even from a hospital bed, despite my body rebelling, I still had my voice. Those were prescribed to me at the time of discharge.

I took a month off from work. One whole month with no alarms and no night shifts. No walking in the hospital halls while half dead. All I hoped for was rest. I didn't spend the month recovering. I spent it unbecoming the shell I had become. For the first time in months, I let myself stop pretending I was okay.

That helped me recover, conserve my energy and strength. That time off helped me adjust to the new life of spit cups and bags, it gave me space to try food items, and the resting period helped the steroid medication work. I spent it unbecoming the version of myself that said, "It's fine. I can push through. Don't worry about me."

That's the woman I had to dismantle. And in her place, I let a quieter woman emerge. One who trusted stillness. But I started to miss being at work. I must say, if we had another financial source, I would not have gone back so soon.

I wasn't receiving any salary during my time off from work, so I contacted my disability insurance. The representative was compassionate and helped me with the application, but he said the payout would take 60 to 90 days. I was broke and needed the money during my time off from work. By the 60 to 90 days payout period, I would likely be back at work and no longer need the disability benefits. Therefore, I cancelled the disability application.

After our wedding in July, my mom went to Scotland to stay with my sister for some time. She was planning to stay there till December. After I left the hospital, I called my mom. We hadn't spoken much. I hadn't wanted her to worry. But when I told her what I'd been through, she changed her ticket. Left Scotland. Flew back to Pennsylvania.

She didn't ask, "Why didn't you tell me?" She just came. And I remembered again: Love doesn't always knock. Sometimes it just arrives.

Lesson: Support doesn't always come from where you expect it. Sometimes it's a nurse with a shared story. Sometimes it's a cousin who brings rice and chicken sauce. Sometimes it's your mother, crossing oceans without asking. And sometimes … it's you. Asking for the pill. Asking for the time off. Asking for your life back.

Support women with hyperemesis gravidarum. This line is to the family members in her life; take up a new job that provides income, unburden her especially financially because the majority of the time, she goes back to work too soon due to financial obligation. And as for the woman, consider trying vitamin B_6 (pyridoxine) and doxylamine, but remember it may not work for everyone. Do not be discouraged. The journey involves trying as many things as possible.

Chapter 10: Nzu

My sisters are known for always eating Nzu. Growing up, I rolled my eyes every time I saw my sisters munching on Nzu. "You know that's just mud with a fancy name, right?" I'd tease.

They laughed, called it a craving. I called it dangerous. The doctor. The rational voice in the room. I was always the one telling them to stop, that I don't see any benefit from eating this. I explained to them that it was likely the cause of their anemia and intermittent constipation. Until I became the one vomiting bile and air and begging for sleep. Until reason couldn't save me anymore.

Nzu is an edible chalk from West Africa, also known as calabash chalk in Nigeria. It is naturally formed from fossilized seashells, although it can also be artificially prepared using clay and mud. Sometimes, it is salted, but I don't understand why anyone would eat unsalted Nzu.

It was always present in the homes of women who had just had a baby. For this reason, you will always find kids visiting such homes so they can get some Nzu.

When I reached the edge, I didn't pray. I didn't Google. I called my eldest sister and asked, "Can you send me some Nzu?"

She laughed and asked, "Have you come to the dark side?" She sent it. The box arrived like contraband. I opened it like a sacred artifact. I held the chalk between my fingers and felt a sense of shame. It was everything I said I'd never need, pressed into the palm of a woman no longer sure of anything except that nothing clinical was working.

I sat on the edge of the bed. Jacob watched me. I raised the chalk to my lips. Then I bit into it, it was a dry, slightly earthy crunch. Finally, it disintegrated into paste, and it soothed me. Not like medicine. Like soil. Like memory.

It helped with my nausea and vomiting. I didn't throw up for six hours. Then twelve. Then a full day. I could sit up without gagging. I could think. For the first time in months, I felt like a mother. Not a patient. So I kept eating it—to the point Jacob was worried that our baby would come out in clay color and that the doctors would panic.

My lips turned white. Jacob stared. "You look like Tyrone," he said, referencing the Dave Chappelle sketch of a crack cocaine user with white lips from using crack. We laughed. It was ridiculous. But we laughed. Even survival needs comedy.

I ate it during rounds at work. I didn't hide it. I broke off pieces during rounds, between patients. Colleagues stared.

Some asked. "What is that?" "Why are you eating clay?" I didn't flinch. "Because it's the only thing that keeps me from vomiting on your shoes."

They didn't laugh. But I meant every word. I ate Nzu to the last day of pregnancy and many weeks beyond.

I wonder now: Did my mother eat it too? My grandmother? Is this what they meant when they said, 'Pregnancy is hard, but you'll get through it"?

Maybe we've all been getting through it with chalk-stained mouths. Maybe we survive by passing down the tools, even the dangerous ones, in silence. Maybe the silence itself is a form of love.

Lesson: Nzu is used as an antacid, antidiarrheal, nutritional supplement, traditional medicine, spiritual practices, and morning sickness. Studies in rats have shown that exposure can lead to negative effects such as decreased maternal weight gain, impaired fetal development, and possible pregnancy loss. It contains toxic heavy metals and other pollutants, making it potentially harmful to consume.

Yes, Nzu has been studied. Yes, it contains lead, arsenic, and aluminum. Yes, it's toxic. And yes, I kept eating it. Because science doesn't always soothe. Because even when you know the side effects, desperation makes a compelling case. Because I didn't want my baby to die. And I didn't want to die either. And for a brief window in time, Nzu let me live.

I justified my use of Nzu by stating that studies were in rats, and that I am not a rat, and that it helped me not to vomit. Additionally, I did not experience further weight loss; in fact, I started gaining weight toward the end of pregnancy. I gained a significant amount of weight, leading to a diagnosis of gestational diabetes. I am also worried about potential neurological effects on my baby, but thankfully, so far, no issues have been observed.

https://www.tandfonline.com/doi/full/10.1080/02772248.2015.1110157#:~:text=Citation%202011).%20Thus%2C%20consumption%20of%20large%20quantities,health%20and%20that%20of%20their%20unborn%20child.

Chapter 11: Bitter Kola

African bitter kola, also known as Garcinia kola, is used as a medicinal agent, as a stimulant, to aid digestion, boost the immune system, and provide a natural energy boost. Side effects that have been reported include increased blood pressure, insomnia, nervousness, and jitters. Pregnant and breastfeeding women are generally advised to avoid bitter kola due to the potential risks to the fetus or infant.

I remembered seeing my mom eat bitter kola when I was growing up. I remembered she ate it whenever she ate something that is not spicy that made her nauseous. I don't remember when I first saw her do it. Maybe it was in the kitchen, after a meal that made her queasy. Maybe it was after a long day, when her eyes looked tired but her hands were steady. She didn't make an announcement, she didn't slip it into a ritual, it was simply there.

She'd pop a bitter kola into her mouth like it was a mint, no ceremony, no warning. It was just something people did when the world inside them didn't sit right. I never asked her why, and she never shared as well. But I remembered.

And now, lying on the floor, too weak to cry and too tired to pray, those memories came rushing back. So I decided to give it a try. I sat with it in my palm for a long time. It was ugly—wrinkled, hard, brown. Not a cure. Not a drug. Just… a seed. I brought it close to my lips, feeling the conflict within. The medical part of my brain screamed: *Stimulant. Unsafe. Toxic.* But the mother in me whispered: *Try, just one bite. If it helps, it helps. And if it does, don't ask for permission.* So I bit down. It was sharp. Bitter. It fought my tongue. But it also quieted something inside me—just enough. I used it as a rescue medication, before and after a meal.

Even now, I keep one in the house. Like a talisman. Not because I think it will save me. But because it did, once. Briefly. And memory is a stubborn currency. Sometimes we hold onto what worked—no matter what the cost.

Maybe my mother kept things quiet the way women keep most survival strategies—shared only in silences, passed down without confession. Traditions can travel that way, folded into memory rather than spoken aloud. We talk about pregnancy cravings like they're harmless quirks: pickles, ice cream, the occasional midnight runs. But for me, they were forged in urgency.

In a history of women, pain was sidelined, who learned to doctor themselves when the system wouldn't or couldn't. Maybe this is a way of keeping the next generation from seeing just how much endurance costs.

Lesson: I won't recommend bitter kola. Not officially. Not ethically. It's harsh on the teeth. It raises blood pressure. It isn't safe in pregnancy. But neither is despair. Neither is starvation. Neither is vomiting until you see blood. And so I used it. Briefly. Secretly. Carefully. And then I stopped. Survival is full of contradictions. And the hardest part is knowing when to let go of what once saved you. I feel very lucky that it helped me with my vomiting.

I never asked my mother what bitter kola did for her. But now I think I understand.

It wasn't about digestion. It was about defiance—a refusal to surrender when the body said no. We all have our weapons. Mine, for a time, was bitter and brown— and fit in the palm of my hand.

https://www.webmd.com/vitamins/ai/ ingredientmono-937/cola-nut

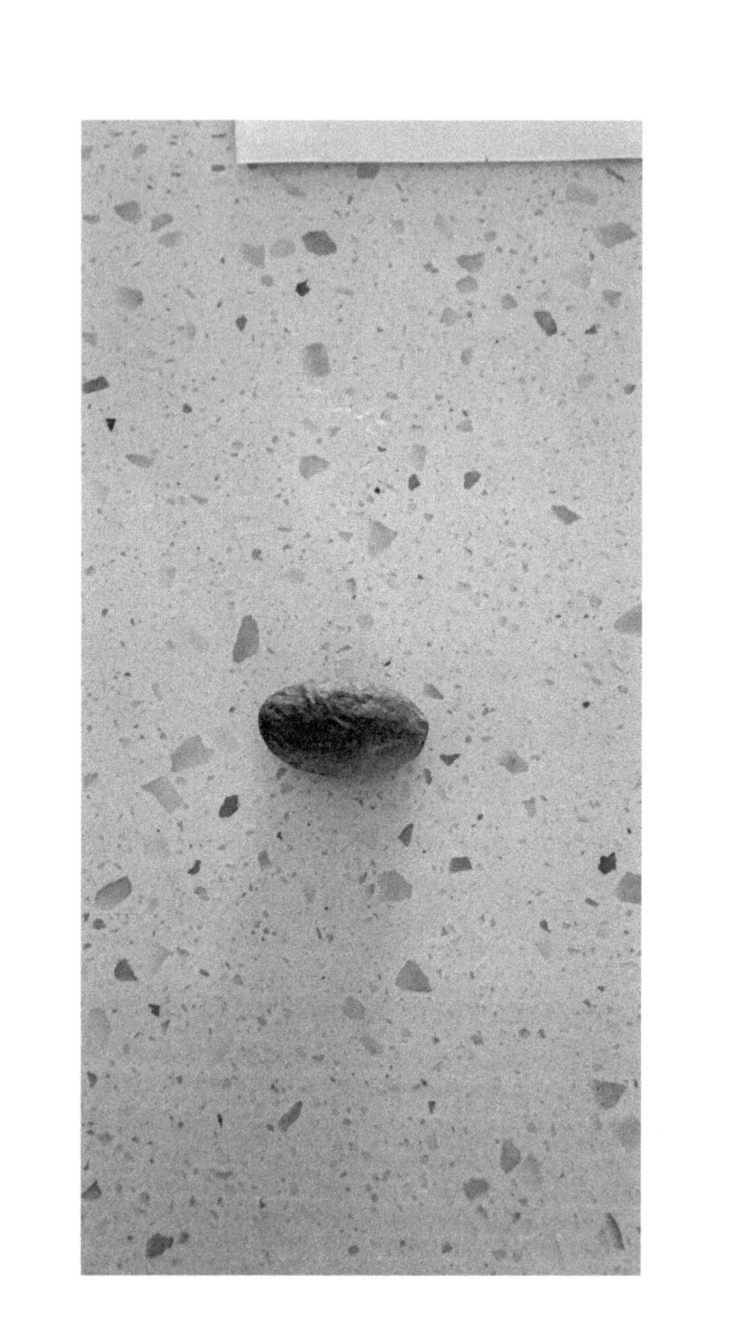

Chapter 12: Gestational Diabetes

They wanted me to celebrate.

"You've gained weight!" they said at my OB appointment.

After months spent shrinking and losing, this was supposed to be good news. Now, at last, my body was making room for someone else. For a brief moment, food was no longer the enemy.

When I started eating, boiled white rice was my main dish. After months of vomiting, it was the first thing I could eat without fear. It was plain. Predictable. A blank canvas my stomach accepted. Every bite felt like a victory, and for days I let myself believe in the miracle of nourishment. Until it became a problem. Until it became … too much.

Apart from this, my snacks were fresh raw coconut. I ate these a lot. My drink was Topo Chico.

Time came for gestational diabetes test. I was asked to monitor my fasting blood glucose every morning for seven days. When I returned my blood glucose level, I was diagnosed with gestational diabetes. My glucose was greater than 95. Another diagnosis. Another chart to monitor. Another way to be told, "You're not doing this right." I stared at the glucometer. 97. Just two points over. But in this world, two points might as well be a mile.

My OB-GYN stated that she sees this all the time: Her hyperemesis gravidarum patients end up with gestational diabetes. I was referred to the gestational diabetes clinic. I met with the nutritionist. She was kind, organized, and full of lists.

"Let's get some protein in. Cut back on rice." I nodded, even as I felt something inside me shrinking. I had just started enjoying food again. Now it was back to restriction. Back to fear. Back to reading labels like they were death sentences. It felt too cruel. After months of famine, my body finally wanted to feast, and now, I was told to ration again.

They understood that my palate was a labyrinth of restrictions, a maze of food items I couldn't navigate. We began exploring new territories, starting with peanut butter and eggs, aiming to forge a path toward nourishment with less rice, taking small, frequent forays. Our map was the diet itself, a quest to tame the gestational beast without resorting to the invasive tool of insulin. I nurtured a tentative friendship with peanut butter, yet eggs remained an unscalable wall.

The clinic's advice was to walk after dinner, a gentle pedal stroke in an effort to soothe the journey, yet this was a trail I never fully traveled. I slowly welcomed fruit into my voyage, a mango shimmering like a distant star, promising sweetness but delivering a storm that bloated fiercely enough to steal my breath. Still, I clung to its memory, soft, luminous, sweet like a land I longed for but could never return to. For me, pregnancy was a voyage across a forbidden continent, a land of luscious fruits that could never be fully tasted.

Then one morning, the air was sharp, the kind that prickles your skin even indoors. I sat at the kitchen table with my elbows on the wood, staring at the cup of tea cooling in front of me. The steam had thinned into nothing, but I couldn't bring myself to drink it. My stomach felt like a stranger, sometimes quiet, sometimes threatening revolt without warning. The faint hum of the refrigerator filled the silence, along with Jacob's soft movements in the next room.

When I finally looked up, Jacob was there, leaning on the doorway like he always did. His eyes met mine, steady and searching. He didn't try to fill the silence with empty reassurances; he knew they wouldn't land. Instead, he asked softly, "What do you need right now?"

I didn't have an answer, not one that could be put into words. So I just whispered, "Stay." And he did. He crossed the room, pulled out the chair beside mine, and sat until the tension in my shoulders eased.

For gestational diabetes, I had to check my blood glucose levels via a finger stick first thing in the morning, two hours post breakfast, two hours post lunch, and two hours post dinner. Four times a day, I stabbed my finger. Morning. After breakfast. After lunch. After dinner. The blood never bothered me. What did? The waiting. The judgment in the numbers. Fasting glucose: 96. Post-meal: 122. Each number felt like a verdict. *Motherhood, pass/fail.*

The goal fasting glucose ≤5-5.3 mmol/l (90-95 mg/dl), and either one-hour post-meal ≤ 7.8 mmol/l (140 mg/dl), or 2-hour post-meal ≤ 6.7 mmol/l (120 mg/dl).

https://pmc.ncbi.nlm.nih.gov/articles/PMC4404472/#:~:text=The%20target%20glycemic%20goals%20for,(120%20mg%2Fdl).

I did my best to achieve the right numbers. I tried peanut butter. It stayed down. Eggs made me gag. I stopped trying to be perfect and started trying to be honest. There were nights I cried over crackers. Days I skipped testing because I couldn't bear one more "too high." But I kept trying because that's what mothers do.

My baby was monitored closely with frequent ultrasound by a specialized maternal-fetal medicine team. Every ultrasound was a silent negotiation. Would she be too big? Too small? Would they induce early? Would this diagnosis mean something was wrong, again? But every time, she waved. Kicked. Grew. She was fine. It was I who couldn't breathe.

She was gaining appropriate weight, with no deficits or concerns. We were scheduled for induction March 28th-29th.

I also had abnormal thyroid hormone levels during pregnancy that were monitored and rechecked after delivery. It has now gone back to normal levels.

There were days when I imagined what it would be like to look back on all this, to tell the story from the other side. In those moments, I could almost see her, the future child I hadn't met yet, the one I kept choosing in small, stubborn ways every day. Sometimes that image was enough to keep me moving, even if moving meant only sitting upright for an hour.

Jacob would sometimes catch me staring into the distance and ask, "Where'd you go just now?"

"I was with her," I'd answer.

And he'd nod, as if he knew exactly what I meant.

Lesson: Gestational diabetes isn't just about blood sugar. It's about constant correction. It's about having come through fire and now being told, "Careful, you're burning again." The experts say there's no link between hyperemesis and gestational diabetes. But I lived both. Back-to-back. And in my body, they were sisters. I believe there is a link, and it needs to be studied further, rather than being ignored.

Sometimes, survival is permission to eat, sometimes it's permission to rest, or to fail. But remember, it is always about forgiving yourself for the ways your body was just trying to survive.

Chapter 13: Full Belly

By the time my belly became full, the violence had stopped. The vomiting, the lines in my arms, the burn in my throat, everything was gone. Or maybe not gone, but hiding.

I was upright, could stand without swaying. Walking. Eating. Breathing. These were no longer assumptions—they were luxuries. I had made it to the third trimester. My belly was round, solid, undeniable. I should have been celebrating. I was finally the pregnant woman people expected. I had waited so long for this body. And now that it was here, I didn't recognize it.

My maid of honor's wedding was in December in Puerto Rico and I was due in late March or early April. During our time in Puerto Rico, friends did not know I was pregnant. They noticed "the face was fuller," but could not see the belly until the wedding day, when I wore a tight dress for the occasion.

After December, I started to gain weight over the last two to three months. The weight gain was rapid. I gained a total of fifty-six pounds.

I no longer feared food. Every bite was permission. Every swallow was joy. I ate rice without guilt. Cucumber as my water. Peanut butter without shame. But mango—I still couldn't. It stayed on my no-list, not because of diabetes, but because it reminded me of everything I lost. Sometimes we keep our ghosts on the menu.

I waddled sometimes even. Leaned. I cursed every staircase. But I smiled when strangers glanced at me. Let them stare. I was no longer the woman vomiting in parking lots. I was the woman with life inside her. I had become visibly pregnant— and that visibility felt like a trophy.

I was ready for the induction and could not wait. We had no formal pregnancy pictures to show off the bump because of everything that has happened. I was so sick and had no desire to do the things other pregnant women do to prepare, such as a pregnancy photoshoot, shopping for baby things, and setting up the baby room.

My work unit medical director asked for a meeting outside of work. I wondered, *What did I do now? What trouble am I in now?* It turned out she was just checking on me and wanted to show me stores around town. The walk through the store, looking at baby items, inspired me to buy things, to start ordering items and prepare for the baby. I had been preparing to die but since we were not dying, we might as well start preparing to live. Crib, clothes, baby bottles, etc. I also decided to pose by our bedroom mirror just to get at least one pregnancy photo.

I had to study and prepare for my Neurocritical Care board exam. Prior to getting pregnant, I had planned study weeks. I had planned time off from work to study and take the exam, but since I had used my time off for hyperemesis, I could not take another set of time off.

Writing this now, I cannot explain when or how I studied. The only thing I remember is the exam day. Days leading to the exam, I wondered if I should reach out to the examining board and ask for accommodations because I was too sick to sit still, quietly for five hours.

I decided not to reach out to them. I did not want pity or disappointment. This would also be the second time I took this exam; I failed the first attempt in 2021. Back then, I didn't succeed because I fixated on a few questions and didn't move on, so I didn't answer the remaining ones. Additionally, I was caring for my nephew, who was seriously ill in the hospital just before the exam. As you can see, I've already used up my excuses. This time, I am determined to pass. I did not request any extension or special arrangements this year, in 2023.

On the day of the exam, while sitting in my study, which I would soon be turning into a nursery, I told the proctor that I was pregnant, and I explained I have a spit cup into which I'll be spitting frequently, some clay rocks (Nzu) that I need to eat constantly to avoid jumping up and vomiting, and Topo Chico to sip. The proctor agreed, and I showed them all of these items. Then the exam commenced.

During the exam, I moved as quickly as I could, didn't dwell on one question, kept moving, and made sure to see and answer every question. During the break, half way through the exam, I laid on the floor. When the exam resumed, I sat back up. I finished all the questions. Glory to God.

In December, the result came out, and I passed. I am now a board certified Neurocritical Care Physician. Words can not explain my joy. I passed while dealing with the most difficult thing I have ever done in my life—being pregnant.

I reached out to my fellowship training director about my symptoms and how I would like to study this and possible treatment in a lab. He sent me research papers about HG. He encouraged me, saying, "Soon you will be holding your baby in your hands, hang in there." I read the research papers and contacted the authors. They were very gracious. They responded. They were happy to discuss HG with me. The main author called via video call. She was a breath of fresh air. She told me her own story and how she came about researching HG. She introduced me to HER foundation. There were numerous resources available on their website. I had a great feeling of a supportive environment.

It was great to see high functioning women with similar pregnancy journeys. I am not alone.

Lesson: Happiness is hard to find when you feel afraid, worried, or exhausted. With hyperemesis gravidarum, I was constantly tired and weak. I couldn't experience the joy of pregnancy and missed out on activities and preparations that pregnant women typically enjoy.

The last two months, I knew I had to get active, get some stamina for the D-day, find some stress relieve activity. I had a pregnancy massage. I attended a few pregnancy yoga classes, and I focused on stretching and finding joy.

Chapter 14:
Due Date and Induction

I was scheduled for induction on the afternoon of March 28th. I hoped that my friend who is an OB/GYN, would be there. Why? Because I was afraid of being the statistics of black women who die during childbirth in America. It was an unrealistic expectation, to have that friend fly from her state, leave her family, to be here for just my delivery. A girl could wish, right?

March 28th arrived, and I was admitted to the hospital.

The light in the room was dim, the kind of muted yellow that made everything look a little older and more fragile. My back pressed against the cool wall, knees drawn up, arms wrapped around my stomach, not in the protective way you cradle a child, but in the way you hold yourself together when everything inside feels like it's falling apart. The air smelled faintly of antiseptic, layered over the sharp, metallic tang of my own fear.

I could hear the beeping down the hall, machines keeping time in the hospital like a clock I hadn't wound myself. Nurses' shoes squeaked against the polished floor, doors hissed open, curtains swished. My mind cataloged these sounds because focusing on them was easier than facing the thought that had been pressing on me since morning: I don't know if I can keep going.

The OB-GYN attending on call explained everything very well. We were very informed by her explanation, and her technique of performing a pelvic exam was first-class. She stated she would check the cervix again later tonight before she goes home. Oxytocin (Pitocin) started.

At 3 a.m., I started to wonder how far dilated I was, if the dose of oxytocin needed to be increased, and why the attending didn't check me one time like she said before she left. I voiced my concern to the nurse. She informed the night team and a resident came in. To increase the dose, a cervix check will be beneficial in better informing the approach and how things are progressing. So, I agreed for the resident to perform my cervix exam. It was the most painful and rough exam I have ever experienced. It was like we were in a fight, and her way of getting back at me was to perform a rough exam.

I called my department chairwoman telling her about my experience early that morning. Yes, I expected the attending to return like she stated. Yes, I wanted special treatment because I am an attending too. Because I could have done better for them.

When my OB-GYN arrived that morning, she was very upset that the chairwoman was involved. It was very intense. I let her have her say. She was very angry. If there was a way for her to throw me out, she would have done so.

After the epidural by the anesthesia team, the OB-GYN seemed to have calmed down. I finally said my own side of the events and how I could have treated them better if the tables were turned. We decided to finish the day on a good note. She checked my cervix, and I was fully dilated and ready to push. My baby arrived at 5:49 p.m. on March 29th, weighing 7.12 pounds and measuring 19 inches long.

She is healthy. She is beautiful. My mom screamed with joy. Jacob stood beside me, holding my hand, and did not leave my side. My mom went with the nurses to get our baby cleaned.

Because I had gestational diabetes, our tiny baby's blood sugar levels were carefully monitored on that first day, like delicate pulses of hope. Each check was a gentle whisper against the vast uncertainty, and when all her levels remained steady and normal, it felt like a dawn breaking through stormy skies, promising calm. She is truly the Rainbow after the storm—a vivid arc of hope and promise shimmering against the broken clouds. My Rainbow. Our Rainbow.

I went back to work after twelve weeks. One day while at work chewing gum, one of my teeth broke in half. It was a deep break. This was attributed to the months of prolonged vomiting that led to tooth damage. I went to the dentist and was told I needed a filling to fill the hole. After the filling, I kept on having discomfort whenever I ate, so I went back to the dentist. She checked the "bite", made some adjustments, and had me eat a cookie in the office.

It seemed better so I went home, only to start having the discomfort with chewing again. I came back to the dentist, more exams, more checks. She mentioned that everything looks good, that the break was deep, and the fillings just need time to adjust. Made a follow-up appointment to check on things, at that point the discomfort was minimal and the next option that was presented to me was having a tooth crown. So for this appointment I told the dentist that the discomfort has improved significantly, so she said we should leave things the way the are.

As I was leaving the dentist office, I could hear them cheering. Weird, right? I am still having issues with that tooth every now and then.

This experience reflects how circumstances in life can shift over time. Initially, the situation seemed to improve, leading to a sense of relief and a decision to go home. However, the discomfort with the tooth returned, reminding us that progress isn't always linear. Reassessments and delays—like returning to the dentist and awaiting tests—are common in real life, where outcomes often depend on ongoing evaluation and patience.

The decision to leave the issue as it was, despite some improvement, illustrates how solutions might be deferred or adjusted as circumstances evolve. The cheering at the dentist's office could symbolize moments of hope or encouragement that sometimes come unexpectedly, even if the underlying problem persists. Overall, this story exemplifies how life's challenges often fluctuate and require persistent attention and adaptability.

Lesson: Advocate for yourself. Have people in the room who will advocate for you when you cannot. I was terrified about going into labor, about delivery. I did not want to be a statistic of black women who die during childbirth. I was relieved when I met the attending physician on March 28th for induction. I was glad and impressed by her teaching and technique. Then when she left for the day without following up like she stated, I panicked. I worried that my worst fear was going to happen.

When I was told it was time to push, I remembered the mother of Jesus Christ was a teenager who delivered her baby alone in a manger. I prayed, "Holy Mary mother of God, help me push. Hold my hand. Give me the strength you used to have a baby." Throughout the process, I kept on saying, "Hold my hands." "Hold my hands Lord, as am crossing Jordan river, hold my hands." "Hold my hands, as I climb up this mountain, hold my hands."

Our daily bible devotion passage for that day March 29th 2024 reads 1 Peter 3:13-18:

13 Who is going to harm you if you are eager to do good? 14 But even if you should suffer for what is right, you are blessed. "Do not fear their threats[a]; do not be frightened." 15 But in your hearts revere Christ as Lord. Always be prepared to give an answer to everyone who asks you to give the reason for the hope that you have. But do this with gentleness and respect, 16 keeping a clear conscience, so that those who speak maliciously against your good behavior in Christ may be ashamed of their slander. 17 For it is better, if it is God's will, to suffer for doing good than for doing evil. 18 For Christ also suffered once for sins, the righteous for the unrighteous, to bring you to God. He was put to death in the body but made alive in the Spirit.

That verse reminds me of the whole day's event. It encompasses everything that happened in terms of the OB-GYN attendings, resident, me being yelled at hours before going into labor, and delivery. "Who is going to harm you"? "Do not fear their threats; do not be frightened." "Always be prepared to give an answer to everyone who asks you to give the reason for the hope that you have. But do this with gentleness and respect."

Chapter 15: Frenotomy

Our baby is healthy, glory to God. She is delicate and fragile, but I still remember that somehow she was the heaviest thing I had ever carried. Her skin is soft as a petal, her scent a mix of milk and newness.

I still remember how I traced her tiny fingers with my thumb, stunned that they curled instinctively around me, as if she already knew who I was. I felt an ache rise in my throat, a blend of joy and disbelief. This was the same body that had fought me for months, wringing me dry, pushing me to the edge.

When the pediatrician came for her first evaluation at the hospital, I didn't want to let her go. I watched as the pediatrician gently examined her, speaking in calm, practiced tones. She noticed a prominent upper lip frenulum and stated, "No issues here, may need some work when teeth start erupting." The description in the chart: "small cleft in upper gum line" and "moderately inelastic frenulum attached to the tongue." Her words seemed clinical, but my heart tucked them away instantly, because every note, every observation about my daughter felt personal.

Breastfeeding started to become very painful. In the first few days, we met with a lactation consultant, who educated us and demonstrated techniques to help relieve the pain. I cried during the consultation because it was the first time our baby latched well and that there was no pain during the feeding. Going forward the pain returned and intensified. We had a couple more appointments and were referred to a physician lactation specialist.

We met and during her physical exam of our baby, she found a prominent lingual frenulum. She recommended a frenotomy for tongue-tie, also known as ankyloglossia, stating it would stop the pain with breastfeeding.

I struggled to make the decision and went back and forth about whether to proceed with the procedure or not.

I chose to continue breastfeeding despite the pain, trusting it was the best for my baby.

However, I learned that ongoing discomfort could lead to issues like mastitis, vasospasm (which I was already experiencing), nipple trauma, engorgement, and breast thrush.

After talking with a friend who is an ear, nose, and throat doctor, I decided to go ahead with the procedure. It was heartbreaking to see our little one cry afterward and refuse to latch. Fortunately, over time, breastfeeding and the pain both got better, and that brought us a lot of relief.

I still wonder, did the use of steroids caused the small cleft in her upper gum line? Avoiding steroids use prior to ten weeks of pregnancy was to help avoid cleft palate. But as Dr. Fejzo said, "No no no, you cannot think that way. You cannot do this [guilt] to yourself."

Our baby currently has a gap in her teeth. She is doing well and thriving.

Lesson: I cannot prove or disprove if the steroid is the cause of "small cleft in upper gum line" and "moderately inelastic frenulum attached to the tongue." But I am grateful that our baby is healthy. I have read about serious deficits that can and have occurred in some babies from hyperemesis gravidarum.

Chapter 16:
Hyperemesis Gravidarum

It began without mercy. I woke up one morning and vomited before I could even sit up. By midday, it was the same again, and by evening, still no relief. Day after day, the vomiting returned, an unrelenting cycle that made the hours blur together.

I would lie on the bathroom floor, my cheek pressed against the cold tile, so I wouldn't have to crawl far to the toilet bowl. Sometimes, I stayed there for hours. Other times, I lay on the couch, afraid to climb the stairs because movement itself, especially climbing, seemed to trigger more vomiting.

By night, I would drag myself upstairs to our bedroom, stopping first at the toilet bowl before collapsing into bed. This all had been my routine before my miracle arrived.

Hyperemesis gravidarum (HG) is intractable vomiting during pregnancy, leading to weight loss and volume depletion. There doesn't have to be a ketonuria and/or ketonemia. It is an all-day vomiting, day in day out vomiting.

The mother presents with weakness, exhaustion, sometimes dizziness, depression, and in extreme or untreated cases, Wernicke encephalopathy. Risks to the baby include birth defects, neurodevelopmental disorders, increased hospital admission, premature birth, low birth weight, shorter length, and increased risk of testicular cancer in male offspring.

The International Conference on Hyperemesis Gravidarum (ICHG) 2024 unveiled the devastating, far-reaching consequences of this often-dismissed condition. One particularly haunting case detailed the arduous journey of a child born to a mother with HG, a child who has already endured 35 corrective, life-saving surgeries. But perhaps even more chilling was the video shown of a European woman, a face in the crowd, driven to suicide by the relentless torment of HG.

The cost of HG is significant, affecting approximately 0.3%–2.0% of pregnancies, $200-500 million and more annually, loss of income, lost days at work, loss of productivity, loss of work force because many can not go back to work.

The link between HG and adverse child outcomes is still being researched. There have been genes linked to hyperemesis gravidarum, two noted ones are GDF15 and IGFBP7. Investigators have reported fetal production of GDF15 and maternal sensitivity to it both contribute to the risk of HG. The studies found higher GDF15 levels in mother's blood, and these were associated with vomiting in pregnancy and HG. This study found that the vast majority of GDF15 in the mother's blood is from the feto-placental unit. Having low levels pre-pregnancy, then getting high levels during pregnancy, increases the risk of HG. This was supported by β-thalassaemia patients a condition in which GDF15 levels are chronically high (chronically hormonal/genetic stressed state), experience very low levels of nausea and vomiting of pregnancy. It seems the acute risk in GDF15, is a path of HG, while having chronic high GDF15 does decrease the risk of HG. The receptors of GDF15 (GFRAL and RET) are in the hindbrain (pons, cerebellum, and medulla) of the brainstem. One of the functions of this brain location is to make us vomit. For example, when the brain is in trouble due to increased intracranial pressure (brain pressure), the brainstem induces vomiting without nausea. This makes sense why the vomiting in HG is ruthless, because the receptor is in place that naturally causes vomiting, hence anti-nausea medications that are prescribed have no chance, no stand against this intelligently suited system.

GDF15, or Growth Differentiation Factor 15, is a cytokine belonging to the Transforming Growth Factor-beta (TGF-β) superfamily. Its primary biological roles vary depending on the physiological or environmental context, particularly in non-pregnant states and prior to pregnancy. The question arises: What is the main purpose of GDF15 in these conditions? It is logical to assume that GDF15 must serve an important function. Otherwise, it would not have persisted throughout mammalian evolution. Its conservation suggests that it provides some adaptive advantage.

In humans, one well-documented function of GDF15 is to regulate appetite and energy balance. Specifically, elevated levels of GDF15 are associated with reduced food intake, leading to weight loss. This indicates that GDF15 acts as a signal to suppress appetite, potentially contributing to mechanisms of weight regulation and energy homeostasis. Such a role could be particularly relevant in situations requiring energy conservation or in response to metabolic stress.

Interestingly, the function of GDF15 appears to be species-specific. In fish, such as goldfish, research has shown that GDF15 actually promotes food intake rather than suppressing it. Studies involving intraperitoneal administration of GDF15 in goldfish demonstrate increased food consumption, suggesting a role in stimulating appetite in aquatic vertebrates. This dichotomy highlights the complex and context-dependent nature of GDF15's functions across different species.

Overall, GDF15 appears to be a versatile cytokine with divergent roles in different organisms, likely reflecting evolutionary adaptations to their specific environmental and physiological needs. Its conserved presence in mammals underscores its importance, even as its functions continue to be elucidated in various species and contexts.

Other functions: GDF15 assists in glucose and lipid metabolism, and it can improve insulin sensitivity, glucose and lipid metabolism, development of skeletal muscle and bone levels increase in response to stress, including exercise and tissue injury, have both pro-tumorigenic and anti-tumorigenic effects depending on the specific cancer type, and iron metabolism by regulating hepcidin expression.

Even though some experts report no causation between HG and gestational diabetes, because GDF15 increases insulin sensitivity, then maybe the GDF15 in HG is not only increased, but may be defective as well, hence can not perform the functions of a normal GDF15 such as decreasing insulin resistance hence leading to gestational diabetes. This is probably why GDF15 is shown to be increased in cardiovascular disease (CVD) and diabetes—a chronically stressed state. In these diseases GDF15 are defective hence could not combat the constant inflammation of these diseases.

The treatment of HG is currently under investigation, such as a GDF15 blocker for symptomatic relief and to help prevent the negative effects of HG listed in the beginning of this chapter.

Symptomatic treatment include intravenous fluids, thiamine, antiemetics, steroids, and working with a nutrition team to try food items and to evaluate when to start enteral and parenteral feeding.

Experimental symptomatic relief include Mirtazapine, Olanzapine, Gabapentin, and acupuncture. Metformin has been studied for patient's prior to pregnancy to desensitize women to GDF15 so they are no longer hypersensitive to its rise in pregnancy. These are still under investigations.

Abortion is not a treatment. About 4.9% to 15.2% of HG pregnancies end in abortion. Some of these terminations were wanted pregnancies.

While 52.1% considered termination. That is half of all HG pregnancies. This is a staggering number and should concern us all.

Let me tell you a story about HG and abortion. In medical school 2012/2013, I started having abdominal pain and diarrhea. It went on for days, then progressed to constant vomiting. My second older sister suggested eating banana to help with the diarrhea. I had an exam few days later, still with these symptoms. Throughout the exam, I got up multiple times to go use the bathroom.

After the exam, I chose to go the emergency room to see what was the cause of my symptoms. They drew labs and said the blood must have hemolysis because there is no way my potassium is 7 (very high). Labs were redrawn, and potassium was still 7. My partner at that time reminded me that I had been eating lots of banana, hence the elevated potassium.

Other labs returned. I was pregnant. I was worried. I cried. Why? 1) Because I was in medical school and no time to miss classes. 2) These symptoms seem different than what I have seen other pregnant women go through. 3) Maybe the fetus is already deformed from all the ibuprofen I have been taken due to the abdominal discomfort. 4) Yes, there was shame about giving birth before a formal wedding.

I went home, and it was like the flood gate of vomiting opened. I did not leave my couch for one week.

When my partner returned after a week, he was disgusted by my looks and the smell of the apartment. I knew I had to do something. I made an appointment for an abortion.

When my friend came to pick me up, the first words uttered were, "Chidinma you look like a skeleton, is everything ok?"

In the abortion clinic, I informed that I would not be able to keep down the abortion pill, and I asked if there were other options.

They informed me that they always start with the abortion pill "and then go from there."

I took the pill and by the time I walked to the parking lot, I started vomiting. I saw the whole pill come out and into the trash can.

I went back into front office and informed them I just vomited outside. Then they scheduled me for a dilation and evacuation. I had the abortion. The physician was gentle, impersonal, and caused little pain.

As days went by, symptoms resolved, and I started to eat slowly.

Residency training 2016/2017 was a great and supportive experience. I cannot thank them enough. One day I had to call out of work because of abdominal discomfort and vomiting. I bought remedies over the counter, with no improvement. I went to the urgent clinic, lo and behold, found out that I was pregnant. I got to stop finding out that I am pregnant in the emergency room or urgent care clinics.

I had hoped to do it this time around. I had supportive friends. I did not want to be that person who gets two abortions. I tried. I prayed and bargained with God. I asked him to please take these symptoms away, stop the vomiting. "If you won't stop the vomiting, then take the baby and give it to those women who have been praying to you for a baby." Vomiting was still there. I informed the clinic that I can't keep any pills down. But they insisted that their first step is always the pill. I took the pill, but vomited. I returned to the clinic, an ultrasound was performed.

"Oh! it is still there, but it has stopped growing," they said. A dilation and evacuation was scheduled. I had an abortion. Why? Because I couldn't pause residency training. I didn't want to be held back because I missed training due to severe vomiting.

This termination was brutal. The clinic refused to give anything stronger than ibuprofen because a prescription for something stronger had been given to me during the intake appointment, which I left at home and did not fill. So the cramps started, followed by sharp pain, and then I started shaking.

I went back to work that afternoon. My attending physician for that day saw me and mentioned she was looking for me. I had to come clean about my whereabouts. She hugged me and asked me to lie down in the call room. I asked if I was going septic because I was shaking. She said no that I should just get some rest. She was very comforting, and understanding, using her own life stories to demonstrate that everything would be okay.

After that, it was clear that I was not good with oral contraceptives, so I asked for the progestin rod that goes in the arm.

Now in 2023, finding out in the ER again that I was pregnant. Worse symptoms than the first two. This time I have a name for it, hyperemesis gravidarum. This time I reached out for help, and the right people were there and knowledgeable. This time, I have a partner who chooses me when the times get hard. This time I made it to the delivery room.

Post pregnancy, post hyperemesis gravidarum, I noticed that my memory was not what it used to be. It was like I was in a constant brain fog. I could not remember things I once knew or make quick associations that I used to be able to do.

That frightened me, especially since I am in a career that is fast paced, and a lot is dependent on my memory and knowledge. An example, during one of my rounds seeing patients I could not remember the treatment for neuropathic pain. I felt left out, like I was stuck again and don't belong even after passing the Neurocritical Care board exam.

Today, my memory is better. I am doing better, finding joy, and looking forward to things.

About a week after delivery, I took pictures of all the spit cups and then disposed of them.

While writing this book, I attended a church women's conference where the teacher mentioned "finding the good stuff in the hard stuff." The good stuff for me were glimpses of Jacob's true character; the guiding stars of the physicians, my colleagues, my bosses, and nurses; and finally, the precious gem of our baby.

To anyone enduring HG: You are not weak. You are not broken. The darkness may feel endless, but you are still here. Sometimes the "good stuff" is small: a kind nurse, a day without vomiting, the sound of your baby's heartbeat, the warmth of sunlight through the window after a night of storms, or the steady hand of someone who refuses to let go of you. I choose you.

To the medical providers encountering these patients, be patient, be kind, be knowledgeable, stay up to date, investigate, research, and listen to the patient because you might be the factor between delivery verse termination of pregnancy.

When my daughter smiles, crooked and gummy, as if she knows the battles we've fought, I remember how Jacob chose me and how I chose her before I knew her. I chose her when my body screamed for surrender. I chose her when my soul was silent.

And somehow, in her gaze, I believe, she chose me too. I cherish every moment, knowing that love is the quiet strength that will hold us together, forever.

References

1. Nnorom, I. C. (2015). Major and minor element contents of calabash clay (nzu) from Abia State, Nigeria: evaluation of potential intake benefits and risks. Toxicological & Environmental Chemistry, 98(2), 149–166. https://doi.org/10.1080/02772248.2015.1110157

2. Aprioku JS, Ogwo-Ude EM. Gestational Toxicity of Calabash Chalk (Nzu) in Wistar Rats. Int J Appl Basic Med Res. 2018 Oct-Dec;8(4):249-252. doi: 10.4103/ijabmr.IJABMR_412_17. PMID: 30598913; PMCID: PMC6259302.

3. Moses BE, Emma EJ, Christopher CM, Enobong I B, Theresa BE. Effect of calabash chalk on the histomorphology of the gastro-oesophageal tract of growing wistar rats. Malays J Med Sci. 2012 Jan;19(1):30-5. PMID: 22977372; PMCID: PMC3436492.

4. Alfadhli EM. Gestational diabetes mellitus. Saudi Med J. 2015 Apr;36(4):399-406. doi: 10.15537/

smj.2015.4.10307. PMID: 25828275; PMCID: PMC4404472.

5. Jennings LK, Mahdy H. Hyperemesis Gravidarum. [Updated 2023 Jul 31]. In: StatPearls [Internet]. Treasure Island (FL): StatPearls Publishing; 2025 Jan-. Available from: https://www.ncbi.nlm.nih.gov/books/NBK532917/

6. Fejzo M, Rocha N, Cimino I, Lockhart SM, Petry CJ, Kay RG, Burling K, Barker P, George AL, Yasara N, Premawardhena A, Gong S, Cook E, Rimmington D, Rainbow K, Withers DJ, Cortessis V, Mullin PM, MacGibbon KW, Jin E, Kam A, Campbell A, Polasek O, Tzoneva G, Gribble FM, Yeo GSH, Lam BYH, Saudek V, Hughes IA, Ong KK, Perry JRB, Sutton Cole A, Baumgarten M, Welsh P, Sattar N, Smith GCS, Charnock-Jones DS, Coll AP, Meek CL, Mettananda S, Hayward C, Mancuso N, O'Rahilly S. GDF15 linked to maternal risk of nausea and vomiting during pregnancy. Nature. 2024 Jan;625(7996):760-767. doi: 10.1038/s41586-023-06921-9. Epub

2023 Dec 13. PMID: 38092039; PMCID: PMC10808057.

7.   Gurtan AM, Khalid S, Koch C, Khan MZ, Lamarche LB, Splawski I, Dolan E, Carrion AM, Zessis R, Clement ME, Chen Z, Lindsley LD, Chiu YH, Streeper RS, Denning DP, Goldfine AB, Doyon B, Abbasi A, Harrow JL, Tsunoyama K, Asaumi M, Kou I, Shuldiner AR, Rodriguez-Flores JL, Rasheed A, Jahanzaib M, Mian MR, Liaqat MB, Raza SS, Sultana R, Jalal A, Saeed MH, Abbas S, Memon FR, Ishaq M, Dominy JE, Saleheen D. Identification and characterization of human GDF15 knockouts. Nat Metab. 2024 Oct;6(10):1913-1921. doi: 10.1038/s42255-024-01135-3. Epub 2024 Sep 26. PMID: 39327531.

8.   Kleinert M, Clemmensen C, Sjøberg KA, Carl CS, Jeppesen JF, Wojtaszewski JFP, Kiens B, Richter EA. Exercise increases circulating GDF15 in humans. Mol Metab. 2018 Mar;9:187-191. doi: 10.1016/j. molmet.2017.12.016. Epub 2018 Jan 17. PMID: 29398617; PMCID: PMC5870087.

9. https://www.hyperemesis.org/research/genetics-faq/

10. https://www.sciencedirect.com/science/article/pii/S0753332224006930#:~:text=In%20both%20cancer%20and%20chronic,of%20GDF15%20in%20this%20condition.

11. Baek SJ, Eling T. Growth differentiation factor 15 (GDF15): A survival protein with therapeutic potential in metabolic diseases. Pharmacol Ther. 2019 Jun;198:46-58. doi: 10.1016/j.pharmthera.2019.02.008. Epub 2019 Feb 18. PMID: 30790643; PMCID: PMC7196666.

12. Dong XC, Xu DY. Research Progress on the Role and Mechanism of GDF15 in Body Weight Regulation. Obes Facts. 2024;17(1):1-11. doi: 10.1159/000535089. Epub 2023 Nov 21. PMID: 37989122; PMCID: PMC10836939.

13. Eddy AC, Trask AJ. Growth differentiation factor-15 and its role in diabetes and cardiovascular disease. Cytokine Growth Factor Rev. 2021 Feb;57:11-18. doi: 10.1016/j.

cytogfr.2020.11.002. Epub 2020 Dec 1. PMID: 33317942; PMCID: PMC7897243.

14. https://www.sciencedirect.com/science/article/pii/S0002937822002496

15. Nijsten K, Koot MH, Bais JMJ, Ris-Stalpers C, van Eekelen R, Bremer HA, van der Ham DP, Heidema WM, Huisjes A, Kleiverda G, Kruizenga H, Kuppens SM, van Laar JOEH, Langenveld J, van der Made F, Papatsonis D, Pelinck MJ, Pernet PJ, van Rheenen-Flach L, Rijnders RJ, Scheepers HCJ, Vogelvang T, Mol BW, Grooten IJ, Roseboom TJ, Painter RC. Hyperemesis gravidarum severity, enteral tube feeding and cardiometabolic markers in offspring cord blood. Br J Nutr. 2022 Dec 28;128(12):2421-2431. doi: 10.1017/S0007114522000587. Epub 2022 Feb 24. PMID: 35197140; PMCID: PMC9723488.

16. https://www.kcl.ac.uk/news/women-terminate-wanted-pregnancies-due-to-hyperemesis-gravidarum#:~:text=A%20

survey%20of%20more%20than,contemplated%20taking%20my%20own%20life%27.

17. Nana M, Tydeman F, Bevan G, Boulding H, Kavanagh K, Dean C, Williamson C. Termination of wanted pregnancy and suicidal ideation in hyperemesis gravidarum: A mixed methods study. Obstet Med. 2022 Sep;15(3):180-184. doi: 10.1177/1753495X211040926. Epub 2021 Oct 19. PMID: 36262812; PMCID: PMC9574451.

Acknowledgments

With gratitude to Laura Harris and the editorial team at Edioak for their thoughtful editing and guidance.

Thanks to Parris Claytor Balazs of Eventfully Chic by Parris, LLC, for hanging in there with me during the wedding process.

About the Author

Chidinma Onweni, MD, attended Federal Government Girls College (FGGC) Owerri, Imo State, Nigeria, where she completed her secondary education. She relocated to the United States of America to further her education. Dr. Onweni attended Midlands Technical College, in Columbia, South Carolina, where she obtained credits to transfer to a four-year-degree college. As a zealous and passionate student, she enrolled at the University of South Carolina, in Columbia, for her first degree. Her medical school was at the Medical University of South Carolina, Charleston, South Carolina. Dr. Onweni completed her residency with East Tennessee State University Internal Medicine residency, in Johnson City, Tennessee. She completed her Neurocritical Care fellowship at Mayo Clinic, in Jacksonville, Florida. She is currently a practicing Neurocritical Care Physician.

She has authored many medical articles in multiple journals, from Oncology, Palliative, to Neurocritical Care related topics. One of those articles is the important "The Power of Mobile Health: The Girl With the Gadgets in Uganda" doi: 10.1016/j.mayocpiqo.2021.01.001.

Dr. Onweni is a new mom and had hyperemesis gravidarum during her pregnancy, which sparked her search for prevention, treatment, and support of hyperemesis gravidarum. She is a proud member of the Advisory Committee of HER Foundation, https://www.hyperemesis.org, which is committed to research and support of women with hyperemesis gravidarum. Also, Dr. Onweni is the cofounder of Tribute Foundation with the mission of teaching skills to the community and saving lives through education. Visit https://tribute-foundation.org. Email info@tribute-foundation.org.

She is passionate about public health, and she believes health is the wealth of a nation.